by Jay Dale

illustrated by Natalie Ali

a Capstone company — publishers for children

Engage Literacy is published in the UK by Raintree.
Raintree is an imprint of Capstone Global Library Limited, a company incorporated in England and Wales having its registered office at 264 Banbury Road, Oxford, OX2 7DY – Registered company number: 6695582

www.raintree.co.uk

Text copyright © Upload Publishing Pty Ltd 2017

Illustration copyright Capstone/Natalie Ali

Editorial credits
Gina Kammer, editor; Charmaine Whitman, designer; Tori Abraham, production specialist

10 9 8 7 6 5 4 3 2 1
Printed and bound in China.

A Baby Panda is Born

ISBN: 978 1 4747 3162 1

Contents

Chapter 1
Bamboo forest

In China high up in the mountains, Mother Panda was getting ready for the birth of her baby. The mist hung like white sheets among the bamboo plants. It was late afternoon, and the air was chilly and damp. Small animals hurried along the leafy forest floor trying to get home before dark.

Mother Panda could hear the farmers far below her misty mountain home as they cut down large sticks of bamboo.

Chop! Chop! Chop!

Every day these farmers were coming closer and closer to her home. The farmers were cutting down the forest to make room to plant food. Like the animals of the forest, they, too, needed to feed their young ones.

Many hundreds of years ago, large numbers of pandas had lived in the forests. But as more forests disappeared, the pandas had to move higher up the misty mountainside. Their home was shrinking, and they could no longer roam freely wherever they wished.

Mother Panda, like all pandas, ate mostly bamboo in large amounts. But this winter there hadn't been enough. She had eaten some little mice just to stop her hunger. As the farmers came closer and closer to her home in the bamboo forest, there was less food for Mother Panda and others like her.

Chapter 2
Baby Panda

As the evening sky turned from pink to orange to purple, Mother Panda made her den in a hollow tree. She now lay down ready for her baby to be born.

As the full moon rose in the night sky, Mother Panda knew her time was near. The forest animals came out of their homes and peered through the quiet forest. They knew something wonderful was about to happen. This was Mother Panda's first baby, and she was ready to welcome her little one into the world.

The early morning light came through the bright green bamboo. And a tiny baby panda was born. She was as light as an apple and just a little bit longer than a pencil. The baby panda was tiny and pink. She had very little hair and no black and white markings like her mother.

Mother Panda sniffed her newborn baby. The little panda was blind and helpless. Mother Panda moved in closer to her baby. After some time, Baby Panda started to drink her milk.

Over the coming weeks, Baby Panda grew and grew. She drank milk from her mother up to 14 times a day! Baby Panda seemed to be always hungry!

Chapter 3
Growing up

Day by day, Baby Panda grew bigger and bigger. By the time she was one month old, she had soft black and white fur. It kept her warm in the cold mountain air. She had a white face, black ears and two black spots over her eyes. She also had black fur around her back, and all her legs were black, too. Her eyes opened after one month, and she had already begun to crawl. Baby Panda was growing up very quickly!

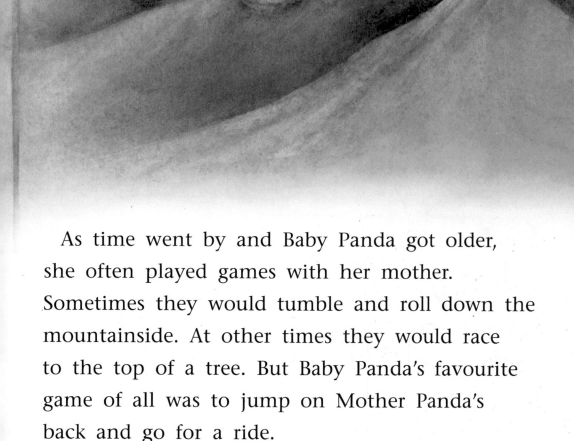

   As time went by and Baby Panda got older, she often played games with her mother. Sometimes they would tumble and roll down the mountainside. At other times they would race to the top of a tree. But Baby Panda's favourite game of all was to jump on Mother Panda's back and go for a ride.

   This little panda had been born in the wild, but would she live there forever?

Chapter 4
Leaving home

Every day the farmers were coming closer and closer. The bamboo forest became smaller. Mother Panda began to eat eggs from birds' nests and fish from the icy river.

Baby Panda was now one year old. She, too, needed a large amount of bamboo to stay alive. She no longer drank her mother's milk.

Baby Panda and Mother Panda searched for bamboo for many hours, day after day. But still it was never enough. Sometimes Baby Panda would eat mushrooms and grass just to fill up her tummy and stop her hunger.

It was at this time that some people from
a large reserve came into the bamboo forest.
Mother Panda didn't know these people
had come to move her and her baby to a
safer place that would have plenty of food.
But that is just what happened! These people
were scientists, and it was their job to help save
the pandas in China. It was their job to help
Mother Panda and Baby Panda survive.

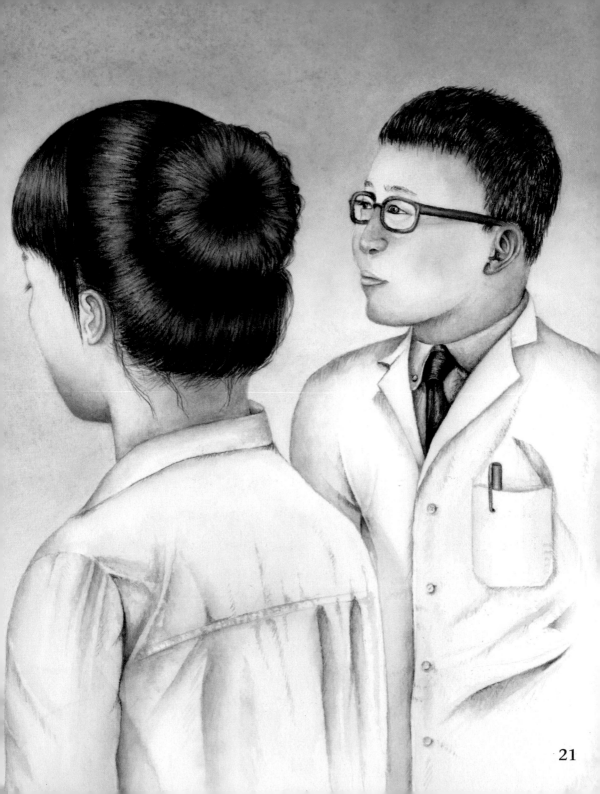

On that day, the scientists took the two pandas to the safety of a special reserve of land. This land was far away from their misty mountain home. But the pandas had everything they needed to survive in a safe place.

So from that day, Mother Panda and Baby Panda were no longer in danger. They were pandas living in a reserve for their own safety.

For Baby Panda it was a fresh start. She had new forests to explore and lots of bamboo to eat.

For Mother Panda everything was a bit
different. She missed the smells and sounds of
her old mountain home. But in their new home,
she and Baby Panda had plenty of food, and
they could wander freely. It was a new and safe
beginning for both of them.